Additional illustrations by Dubravka Kolanovic,
Katie Lovell, Stella Baggot and Abigail Brown
Additional design work by Amanda Gulliver
Photographic manipulation by John Russell
Stories edited by Lesley Sims
Activities edited by Fiona Watt

Some of the material in this book is taken from the following
Usborne titles: Everyday Words, First Picture Action Rhymes,
First Picture Cookbook, First Picture Nursery Rhymes, First Picture 123,
First Numbers, Frank the Farmer, Look and Say Beach, Look and Say Farm,
Look and Say First Words, The Usborne Book of Lullabies,
Usborne Nursery Rhyme Treasury, Very First Dictionary.

First published in 2006 by Usborne Publishing Ltd., 83-85 Saffron Hill, London EC1N 8RT, England.
www.usborne.com. Copyright © 2006 Usborne Publishing Ltd.

The Usborne Baby and Toddler Treasury

Written and compiled by Susanna Davidson
Designed by Hannah Ahmed

Illustrated by Masumi Furukawa,
Jo Litchfield, Cecilia Johannson
and Elena Temporin

Contents

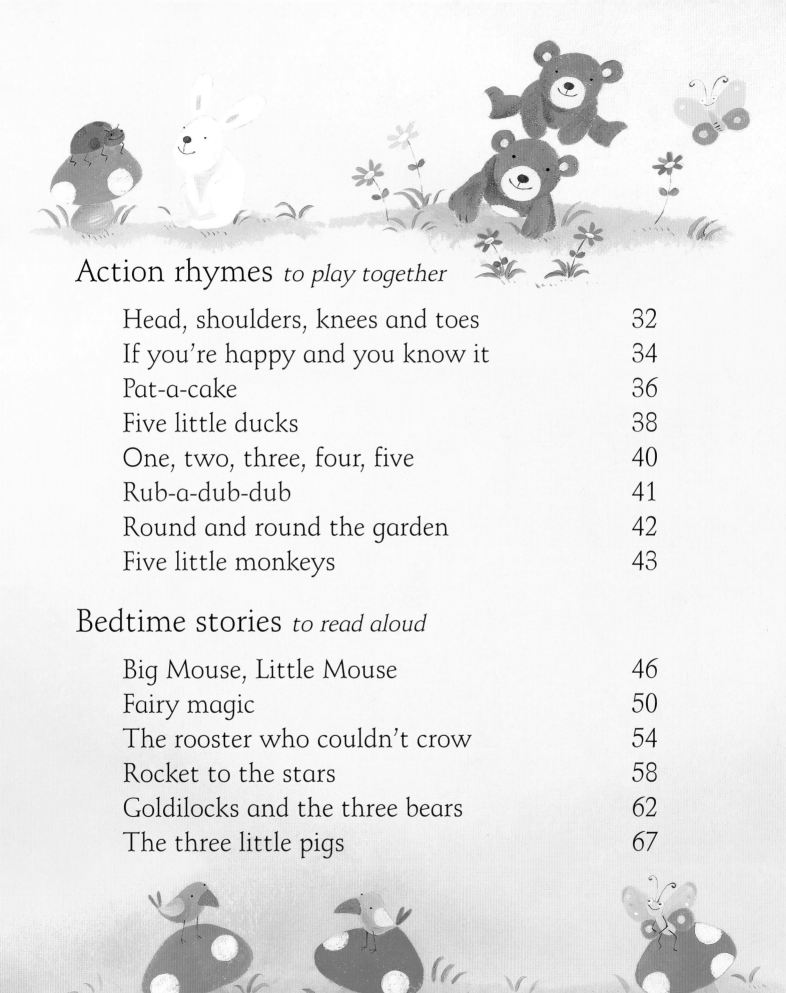

Action rhymes *to play together*

Bedtime stories *to read aloud*

Lullabies *for sleepytime*

Baby and toddler scrapbook *to record special events*

ABCs
and 123s
to say together

Alphabet train

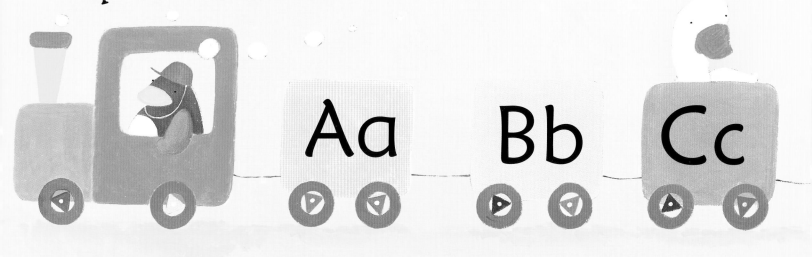

Aa Bb Cc

Ii Jj Kk Ll Mm

Rr Ss Tt Uu Vv

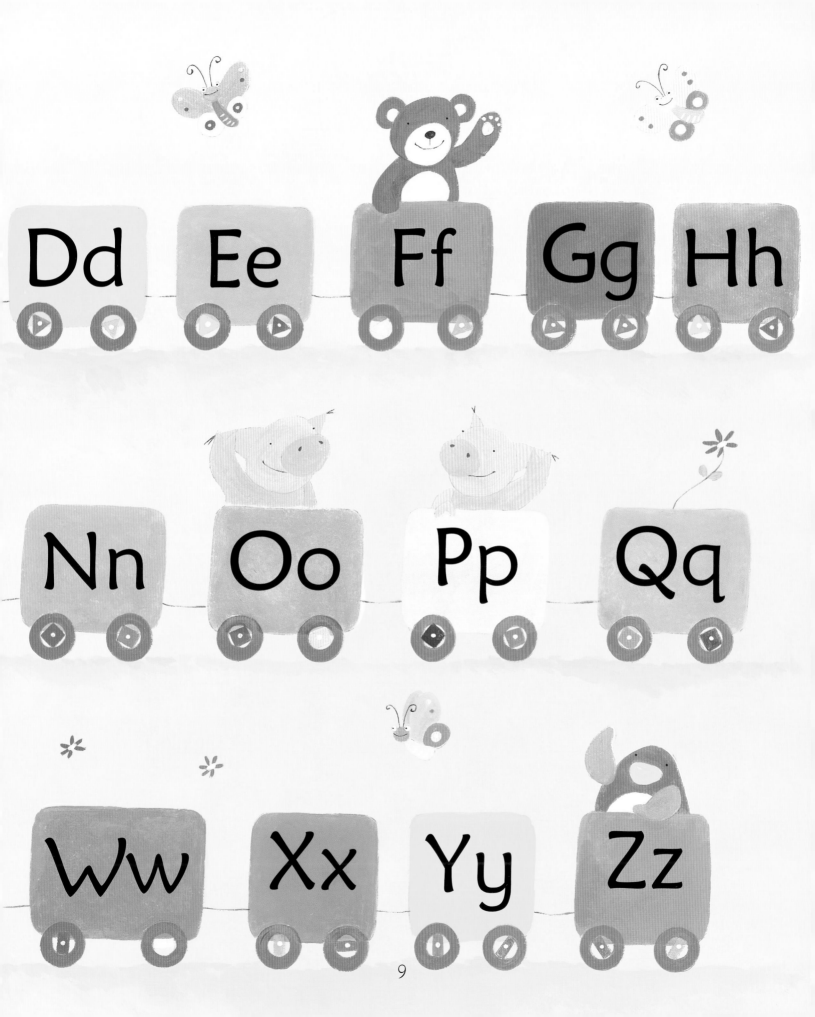

Dd Ee Ff Gg Hh

Nn Oo Pp Qq

Ww Xx Yy Zz

Count to ten

1

2

3

4

5

6

7

8

9

10

Spot the shapes

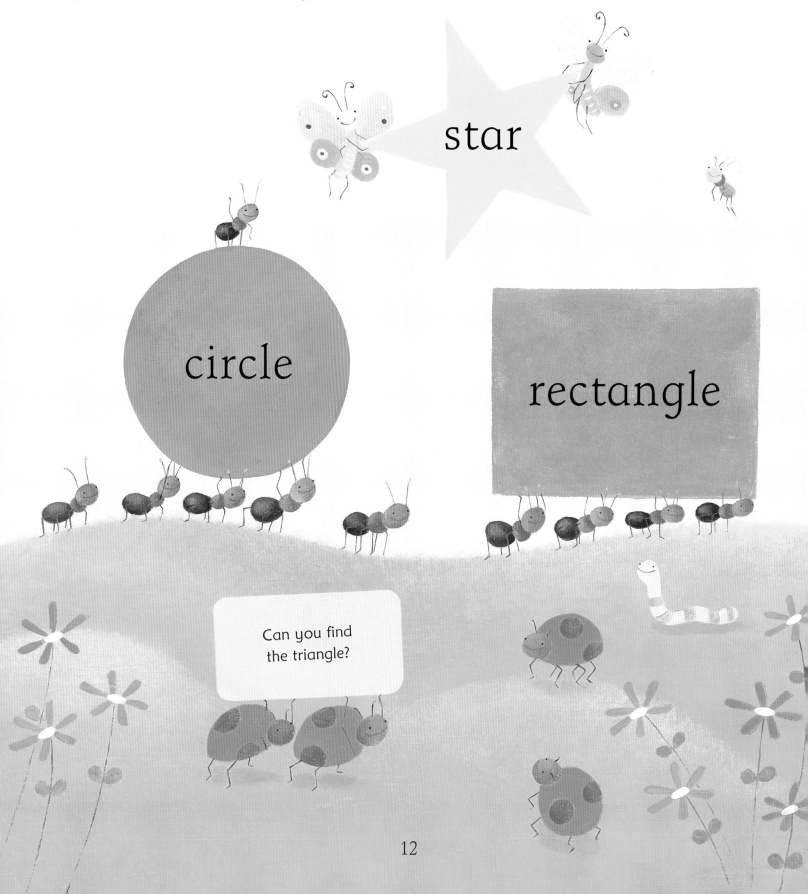

star

circle

rectangle

Can you find
the triangle?

12

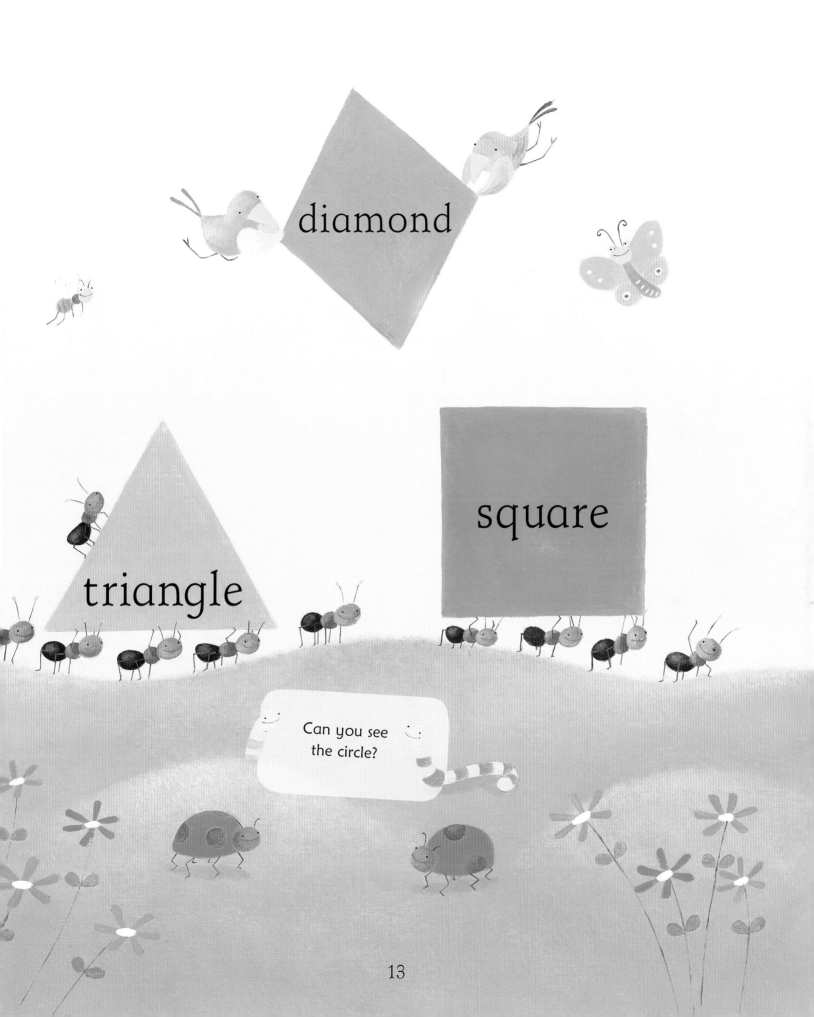

diamond

triangle

square

Can you see the circle?

13

Pink penguin, blue penguin

red

orange

yellow

purple

white

green

black

blue

pink

brown

On the farm

horse

bee

cat

mouse

hen

rooster

frog

duck

sheep

cow

butterfly

dog

pig

This section has activities with nursery rhyme themes. The activities have been broken down into simple, easy steps, with some parts for adults to do, and some that small children will be able to manage with just a little help or even on their own.
Encourage your child to join in where they can.

Playtime
activities

to enjoy together

Twinkly stars

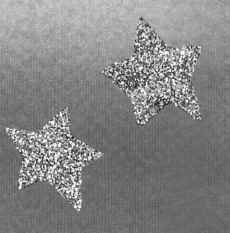

1. Draw lots of star shapes on a blue, black or purple piece of paper.

2. Fill in the shapes with glue. Use a brush or squeeze it from a tube.

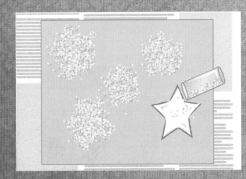

3. Lay the paper on some old newspaper, then sprinkle glitter over the stars.

4. Lift up the paper so the excess glitter falls off. You'll be left with twinkly stars.

Twinkle, twinkle, little star,
How I wonder what you are,
Up above the world so high,
Like a diamond in the sky;
Twinkle, twinkle, little star,
How I wonder what you are.

Paper flowers

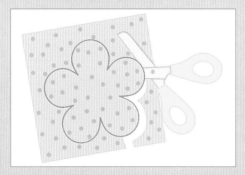

1. Draw the outline of a big flower on a piece of paper and cut it out.

2. Put glue on the back of the flower and press it onto another piece of paper.

3. Then, tear off strips of tissue paper and scrunch them into tiny balls.

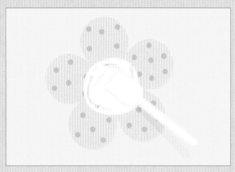

4. Using a brush or glue spreader, put a circle of glue in the middle of the flower.

5. Press the tissue paper balls into the middle of the flower.

6. You can cut a stalk and leaves out of paper and glue them on, too.

Mary, Mary, quite contrary,
How does your garden grow?
With silver bells and cockle shells,
And pretty maids all in a row.

You could add more
flowers to make a
garden scene.

Smiley spiders

1. Dip your finger in paint. Go around and around to make a spider's body.

2. Dip your finger into the paint again and fingerpaint four legs on either side.

3. Let the paint dry, then dip your finger into white paint and print two eyes.

Little Miss Muffet sat on a tuffet,
Eating her curds and whey;
Along came a spider,
Who sat down beside her,
And frightened Miss Muffet away!

4. When the paint has dried, draw a dark dot in each eye with a felt-tip pen.

5. Paint a smiley red mouth with a paintbrush and leave it to dry.

25

Funny faces

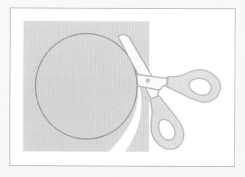

1. Lay a jar lid on a piece of paper and draw around it. Cut around the circle.

2. Put glue on the circle and press it onto another piece of paper.

3. Dip your finger into some paint and print two eyes and a nose.

4. When the paint is dry, spread a thick layer of glue along the top of the circle.

5. Cut off strips of wool, or yarn, and press them onto the glue for hair.

6. When the glue is dry, draw dots in the eyes and a mouth with a crayon.

For fluffy hair, you could use pieces of cotton balls.

You could add
ribbon bows.

Girls and boys, come out to play,
The moon doth shine as bright as day;
Leave your supper, and leave your sleep,
And join your playfellows in the street.

Come with a whoop, come with a call,
Come with a good will or not at all;
Up the ladder and down the wall,
A penny loaf will serve us all.

Painted birds

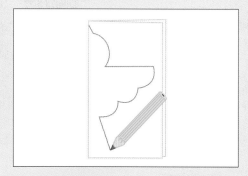

1. Fold a big piece of paper in half and draw half a bird against the fold.

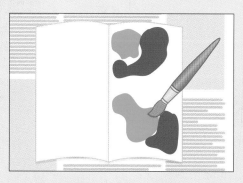

2. Put down newspaper, then unfold the paper. Add big blobs of paint.

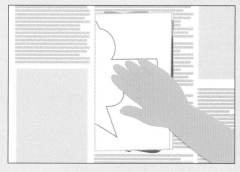

3. Fold the paper again and rub it all over with the palm of your hand.

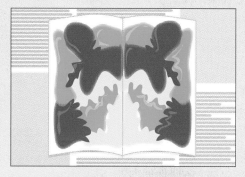

4. Unfold the paper again and leave it until the paint has dried completely.

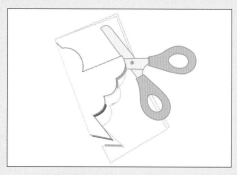

5. Fold the paper in half again and keeping the paper folded, cut out the bird.

6. Then, unfold the paper. Dip your finger into some paint and print two eyes.

Two little dicky birds
Sitting on a wall,
One named Peter,
One named Paul.

Fly away Peter!
Fly away Paul!
Come back Peter,
Come back Paul.

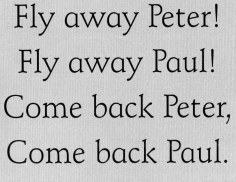

Action rhymes

to play together

Head, shoulders, knees and toes

Head,

shoulders,

knees and toes,

knees and toes.

Head, shoulders, knees and toes, knees and toes.

And eyes... and ears... and mouth... and nose...

Head, shoulders, knees and toes, knees and toes.

If you're happy and you know it

If you're happy and you know it,
Clap your hands.

Clap your hands twice.

If you're happy and you know it,
Clap your hands.

Clap your hands twice.

If you're happy and you know it,
And you really want to show it,
If you're happy and you know it,
Clap your hands.

Clap your hands twice.

Sing the first verse again but replace "Clap your hands" with

"Jump up and down".

For the next verse, replace "Jump up and down" with

"Pat your head".

For the last verse, replace "Pat your head" with

"Shout *hooray*".

Pat-a-cake

Pat-a-cake, pat-a-cake,
baker's man,

Clap your hands together.

Mime holding a pot
and stirring a spoon.

Bake me a cake
as fast as you can.

Pat it,

Pat one hand with your fingers.

36

and prick it,

Prick the palm of your hand with your fingers.

and mark it with "B"

Trace the letter "B" on the palm of your hand.

and put it in the oven for Baby and me.

Mime putting a tray in the oven.

Five little ducks

Five little ducks went swimming one day
Over the hill and far away.
Mother duck said,
"quack, quack, quack, quack."
But only four little ducks came swimming back.

Hold up five fingers.

On the last line, make a swimming action with your hand. Repeat for each verse.

Four little ducks went swimming one day
Over the hill and far away.
Mother duck said, "quack, quack, quack, quack."
But only three little ducks came swimming back.

Hold up four fingers.

Three little ducks went swimming one day
Over the hill and far away.
Mother duck said, "**quack, quack, quack, quack.**"
But only two little ducks came swimming back.

Hold up three fingers.

Two little ducks went swimming one day
Over the hill and far away.
Mother duck said, "**quack, quack, quack, quack.**"
But only one little duck came swimming back.

Hold up two fingers.

One little duck went swimming one day
Over the hill and far away.
Mother duck said, "**quack, quack, quack, quack.**"
And all five little ducks came swimming back.

Hold up one finger.

One, two, three, four, five

On the first line, raise each finger in turn up to five.

On the last line, wiggle the little finger on your right hand.

One, two, three, four, five,
Once I caught a fish alive.
Six, seven, eight, nine, ten,
Then I let it go again.
Why did you let it go?
Because it bit my finger so.
Which finger did it bite?
This little finger on my right.

On the second line, raise each finger from six to ten.

Rub-a-dub-dub

A rhyme for after the bath. Say the rhyme as you rub your child
dry with a towel. On the last line, whip the towel away.

Rub-a-dub-dub,

Three men in a tub,

And who do you think they be?

The butcher, the baker,

The candlestick-maker,

Turn 'em out, knaves all three!

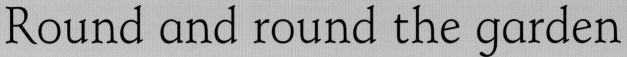

Round and round the garden

As you say the first two lines of the rhyme, trace the tip of your
index finger in a circle on your child's palm. Then "walk" up the arm
with your fingers and tickle your child under the arm.

Round and round the garden,

Like a teddy bear,

One step, two steps,

Tickle you under there!

Five little monkeys

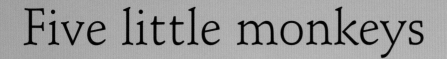

Five little monkeys jumping on the bed,

Hold up five fingers and jump up and down.

One fell off and bumped his head.

Hold up one finger, then rub your head.

Daddy called the doctor and the doctor said,

Pretend to hold up a phone to your ear.

"No more monkeys jumping on the bed!"

Wag your index finger in time to the rhythm.

Repeat the verse with the same actions, replacing "five" with "four", then "three", then "two" monkeys. Then the last verse goes:

One little monkey jumping on the bed,

He fell off and bumped his head.

Daddy called the doctor and the doctor said,

"Put those monkeys back in bed!"

Bedtime
stories

to read aloud

Big Mouse, Little Mouse

"Big Mouse," said Little Mouse, "who's the fastest animal in the jungle?"

"The cheetah," said Big Mouse. "He runs like the wind."

"Big Mouse," said Little Mouse, "who's the slowest animal in the jungle?"

"The sloth," said Big Mouse. "He's slower than a snail."

46

"Big Mouse," said Little Mouse,
"who's the biggest
animal in the jungle?"
"The elephant," said
Big Mouse. "You
can slide down
her trunk."

"Big Mouse," said Little Mouse,
"who's the smallest animal in the jungle?"
"The ant," said Big Mouse.
"She's even smaller than you,
Little Mouse."

"Big Mouse," said Little Mouse, "who's the tallest animal in the jungle?"
"The giraffe," said Big Mouse. "His head is in the clouds."

"Big Mouse," said Little Mouse, "who's the shortest animal in the jungle?"
"The millipede," said Big Mouse. "She's almost flat upon the ground."

"Big Mouse," said Little
Mouse, "who's the quietest
animal in the jungle?"
"Not you!" said Big Mouse. "That's for sure."

"Big Mouse," said Little Mouse,
"who's the loudest animal in the jungle?"
"I AM!" said the lion, with a
great,
big
ROAR!

Fairy magic

For weeks it had done
nothing but rain.
Fairyland looked dark
and gloomy. It was
making everyone sad.

"It's time for some fairy magic,"
said Fairy Red. She flicked her wand
at the flowers, crying, "Let's have
some red!"

"Orange!" said Fairy Orange,
sprinkling spells on the blossom.

"Yellow!" called Fairy Yellow,
spraying sparkles on the sun.

"Green!" said Fairy Green,
flitting through the grass.

"Blue!" said Fairy Blue,
blowing away the clouds.

"Purple!" cried Fairy Purple,
swooping over the mountains.

Rainbow

"Rainbow!" they all called together, flying across the sky.

The rooster who couldn't crow

Croak

Every morning, the rooster on Sunny Farm said Cock-a-doodle-doo! to wake up the farmer. But this morning, he had lost his voice and the animals were getting hungry.

Neigh

"I'll try waking up the farmer," said the horse. And said Neigh! as loudly as he could.

Moooooo

But the farmer didn't wake up.
"He can't hear you," said the
cow. "Let me try!" And the
cow said Mooooooooooo! as
loudly as she could.

Oink
Oink

But the farmer didn't
wake up.
  "He can't hear you," said
the pig. "Let me try!" And
the pig said Oink! Oink! as
loudly as he could.

Baaaaaa

But the farmer didn't wake up. "He can't hear you," said the sheep. "Let me try!" And the sheep said Baaaaaaaaa! as loudly as she could.

But the farmer didn't wake up. Quack Quack "He can't hear you," said the duck. "Let me try!" And the duck said Quack! Quack! as loudly as she could. But the farmer still didn't wake up.

"He can't hear you," croaked the rooster.
"Let's try it together. One... two.... three..."

Mooooo

Neigh

Oink
Oink

Croak

Quack

Baaaaa

All the animals screeched together.
And this time...
the farmer woke up and brought
them all their breakfast.

Rocket to the stars

Teddy and Dolly looked up
at the night sky, at the
shining stars and the
crescent moon.

"I wonder what it's like up there?" said Dolly.
"Me too," said Teddy. "Let's build a rocket
and fly all the way to the moon."

"We need a big
box to sit in."

"And a pointy
roof on top."

"Oh!" cried Dolly.
"I can't see a thing."
So Teddy added
a round window for
Dolly and a square
window for himself.

At last they were ready to go.
Three, Two, One...
Blast off!

They ZOOMED past planets. And did a loop-the-loop around the moon.

"Look at that beautiful star," cried Dolly.

Teddy leaned out the window, and snatched up the star in his paw.

When they got home, Dolly hung the star on the wall. "Look!" she said. "Now we have a star of our own."

Goldilocks and the three bears

Once upon a time there were three bears:

a **great big**
father bear,

a middle-sized
mother bear

and a tiny little
baby bear.

One morning, Father Bear made a large pot
of porridge. "It's too hot to eat now,"
he said. "Let's go for a walk."
But as soon as the bears had gone,
a naughty little girl called
Goldilocks skipped
into their house.

"Mmm! Porridge!" said greedy Goldilocks, sniffing
the air. And she decided to help herself.

She tried the first bowl. "Ow!" she cried. "Too hot!"

She tried the second bowl. "Yuk!" she said. "Too cold."

"Ooh!" she said, as she tried the third bowl. "Just right!"

"Now, where shall I sit?" wondered Goldilocks.
The first chair was too hard. The second chair was too soft.
But the third chair was just right, until...

Whoops!

Goldilocks yawned. Goldilocks stretched. "Time for a nap," she said. So she climbed the stairs to look for a bed. The first bed was too high. The second bed was too low. But the third bed was just right. In no time at all, Goldilocks was fast asleep.

As she slept, the three bears came home.

"Who's been eating my porridge?" said Father Bear, in his great, gruff voice.

"Who's been eating *my* porridge?" said Mother Bear, in her middle-sized voice.

"Someone's been eating my porridge," squeaked Baby Bear, in his tiny voice, "and they've eaten it *all* up."

Father Bear looked down.

"Who's been sitting in my chair?" he growled.
Mother Bear looked down.

"Who's been sitting in *my* chair?" she growled.
Baby Bear looked down. "Someone's been sitting in my chair," he squeaked, "and they've broken it!"

Suddenly, they heard a loud snore.

"Someone's up there!" gasped Baby Bear.
The three bears climbed the stairs.

"Who's been sleeping in my bed?" said Father Bear, in his great, gruff voice.

"Who's been sleeping in *my* bed?" said Mother Bear, in her middle-sized voice.

"Someone's been sleeping in my bed," squeaked Baby Bear, "and she's still there!"

Just then, Goldilocks woke up.
She took one look at the three
bears and screamed.

Then she jumped out of bed,
flew down the stairs and ran out of the house...

...never to be seen again.

The three little pigs

Once upon a time there were three little
pigs who lived with their mother in a
snug little house.

"It's time you had homes of your own," said
Mother Pig one day. "But watch out for the
big bad wolf!"

So the three little pigs packed their bags
and waved their mother goodbye.

Soon they met a man with a bundle of straw.

"Please may I have some straw?" asked the first
little pig. "I want to build a house."

"A straw house won't be strong enough,"
said the second little pig.

"Oh yes it will!" said the first little pig.
And he began to build.

The other two pigs trotted on
until they met a man with a
bundle of sticks.

"Please may I have some sticks?"
said the second little pig. "I want
to build a house."

"A stick house won't be strong
enough," said the third little pig.

"Oh yes it will!" said the second little pig.
And he began to build.

The third little pig trotted on alone until he met
a man with a load of bricks. "Please may
I have some bricks?" asked the third
little pig. "I want to build a house."

The man gave the third little pig
some bricks and the little pig began
to build. "My house will be the
strongest of all," he thought.

Along came the big bad wolf. He stopped outside
the first little pig's house. "Little pig, little pig,
let me come in," he called.

"Oh no," said the first little pig. "Not by
the hair on my chinny chin chin."

"Then I'll huff and I'll puff and
I'll **blow** your house in!" cried the
wolf. And he huffed and he
puffed and **blew** the house in.

The little pig ran away as fast
as he could to his brother's stick house.
But the wolf followed him....

"Little pig, little pig, let me come in," said the
big bad wolf.

"Oh no," said the second little pig. "Not by the hair
on my chinny chin chin."

"Then I'll huff and I'll puff and I'll **blow** your house in!" cried the wolf. And he huffed and he puffed, and he huffed and he puffed, but nothing happened. So he huffed and he puffed again, until at last, he **blew** the house in.

The two little pigs ran away as fast as they could to their brother's brick house. But the wolf followed them...

"Little pig, little pig, let me come in," said the wolf.

"Oh no," said the third little pig. "Not by the hair on my chinny chin chin."

"Then I'll huff and I'll puff and I'll **blow** your house in!" cried the wolf. And he huffed and he puffed. And he huffed and puffed. And he huffed and he puffed until he was completely out of puff.

"Huh!" said the wolf. "I'll just have to find another way in."

Lickety-split, quicker than quick, he jumped onto the roof and down the chimney. He slid down and down...

...the wolf slid so fast he couldn't stop. He fell straight into a pot of water with a great big PLOP!

The third little pig quickly slammed on the lid. "Ha!" said the three little pigs. "By the hairs of our chinny chin chins, we won't be seeing that wolf again!"

Lullabies

for sleepytime

Rock-a-bye baby

Rock-a-bye baby, in the tree top,
When the wind blows, the cradle will rock.
When the bough breaks, the cradle will fall,
Down will come baby, cradle and all.

Bye baby bunting

Bye baby bunting,
Father's gone a-hunting,
Mother's gone a-milking,
Sister's gone a-silking,
Brother's gone to buy a skin
To wrap the baby bunting in.

Golden slumbers

Golden slumbers kiss your eyes,
Smiles awake you when you rise.
Sleep pretty darling, don't you cry,
And I will sing a lullaby,
Lulla, lulla, lullaby.

I see the moon

I see the moon, the moon sees me,
Under the shade of the old oak tree.
Please let the light that shines on me,
Shine on the one I love.
Over the mountains, over the sea,
That's where my heart is longing to be.
Please let the light that shines on me,
Shine on the one I love.

All the pretty horses

Hush-a-bye, don't you cry,
Go to sleepy, little baby.
And when you wake, you shall have
All the pretty little horses.
Blacks and bays, dappled manes,
Coach and six white horses.
Hush-a-bye, don't you cry,
Go to sleepy, little baby.

Sleep, baby, sleep

Sleep, baby, sleep,
Your father tends the sheep.
Your mother shakes the dreamland tree
And from it fall sweet dreams for thee.
Sleep, baby, sleep - sleep, baby, sleep.

Sleep, baby, sleep,
The large stars are the sheep.
The little stars are the lambs, I guess
And the silver moon is the shepherdess.
Sleep, baby, sleep - sleep, baby, sleep.

Baby & toddler scrapbook

to record special events

My first day

I was born on

....

I was born at

....

I weighed ....

My handprint

My footprint

My first moments

I first smiled on ....

I first sat up on ....

I first crawled on ....

My first tooth came on ....

I took my first steps on ....

My first word was ....

My first drawings

My first birthday

Who was at my birthday party?

....

I wore ....

I was given ....

....

My first Christmas

I spent my first Christmas at

....

Who was there? ....

I was given ....

....

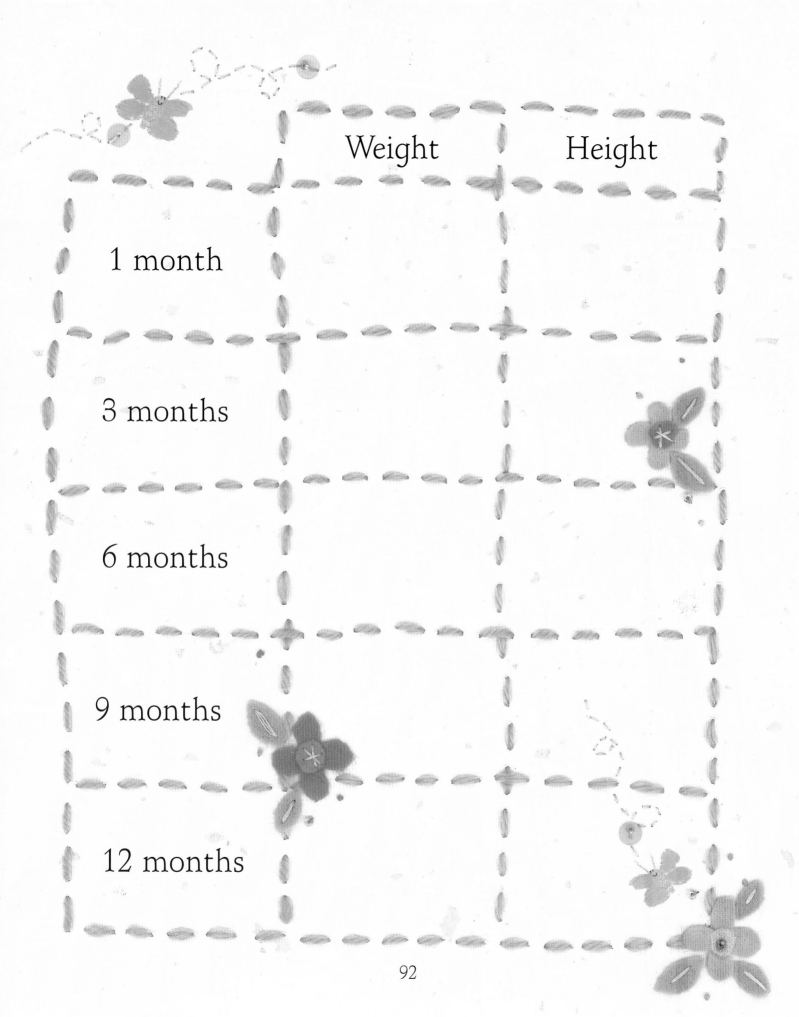

	Weight	Height
1 month		
3 months		
6 months		
9 months		
12 months		

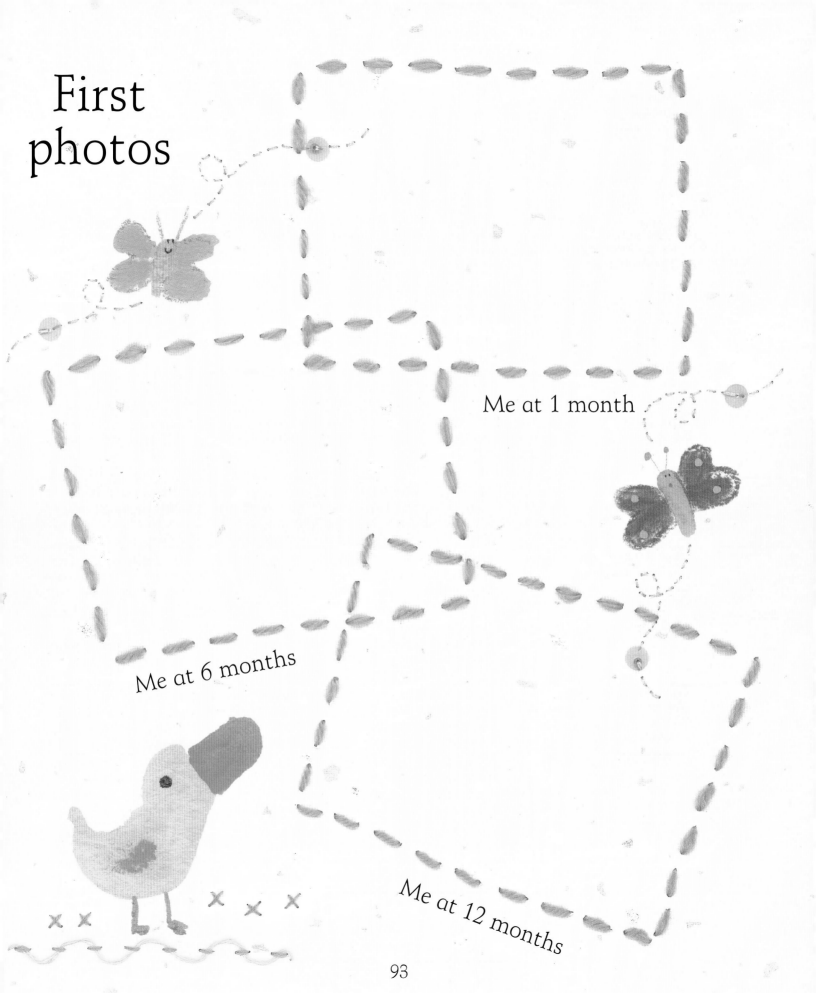

First photos

Me at 1 month

Me at 6 months

Me at 12 months

93

My family tree

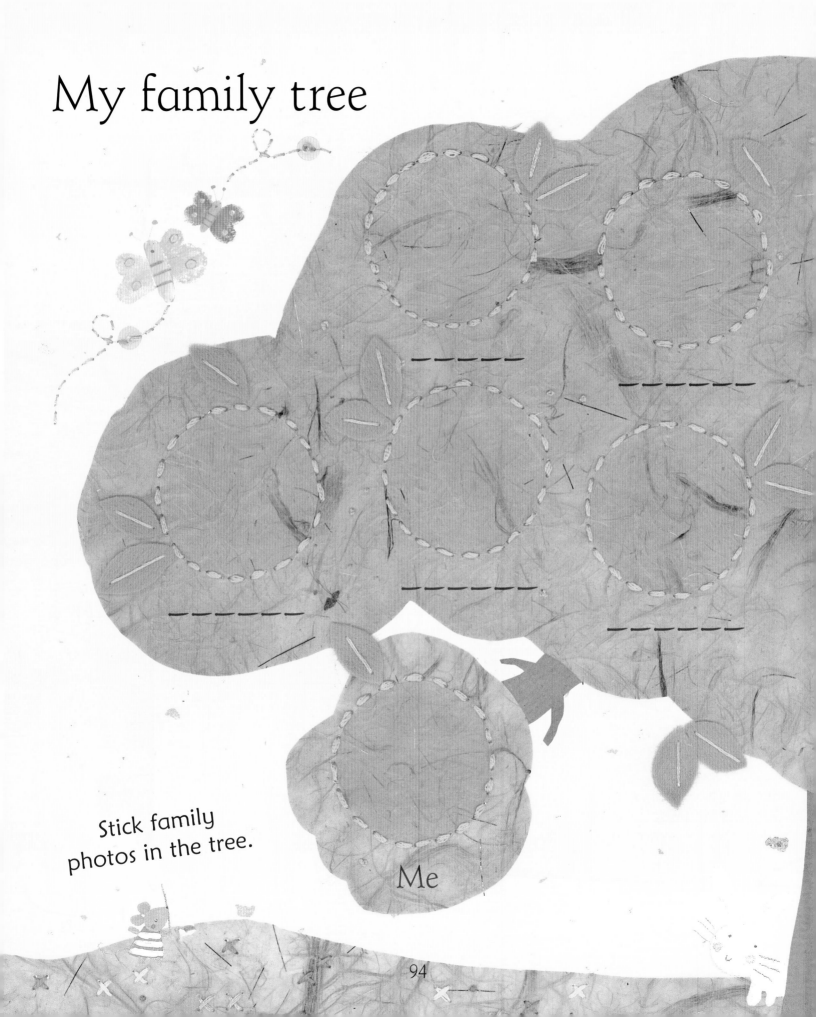

Stick family
photos in the tree.

Me

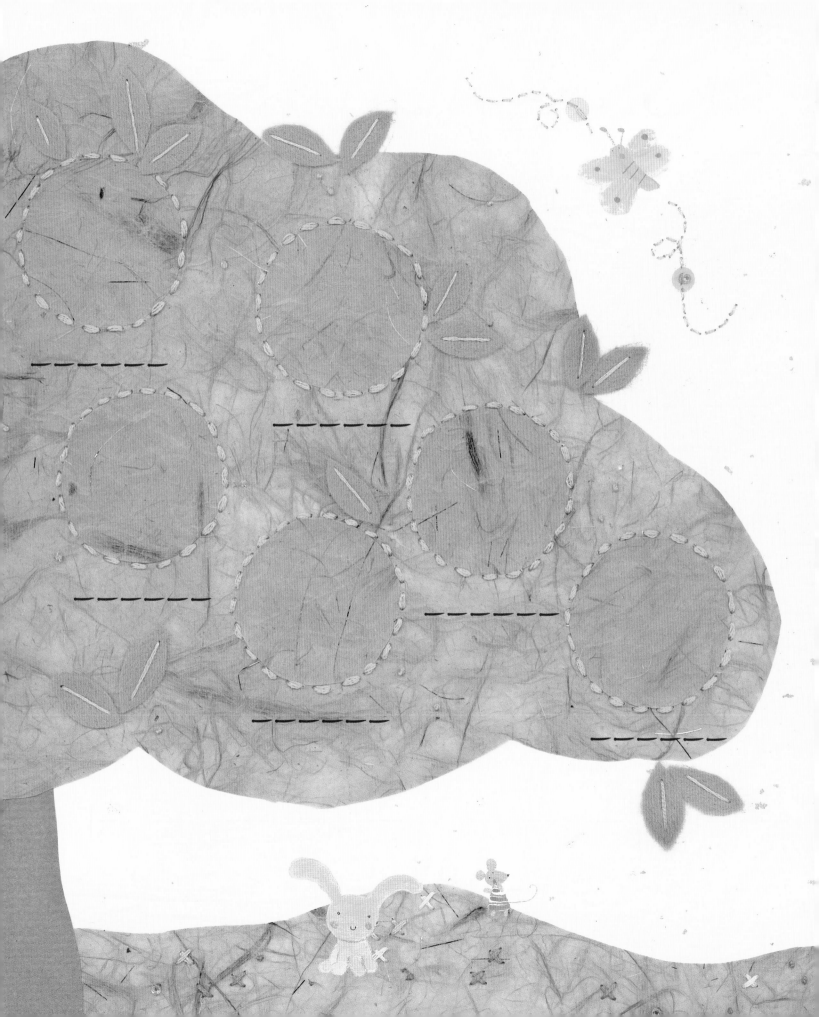

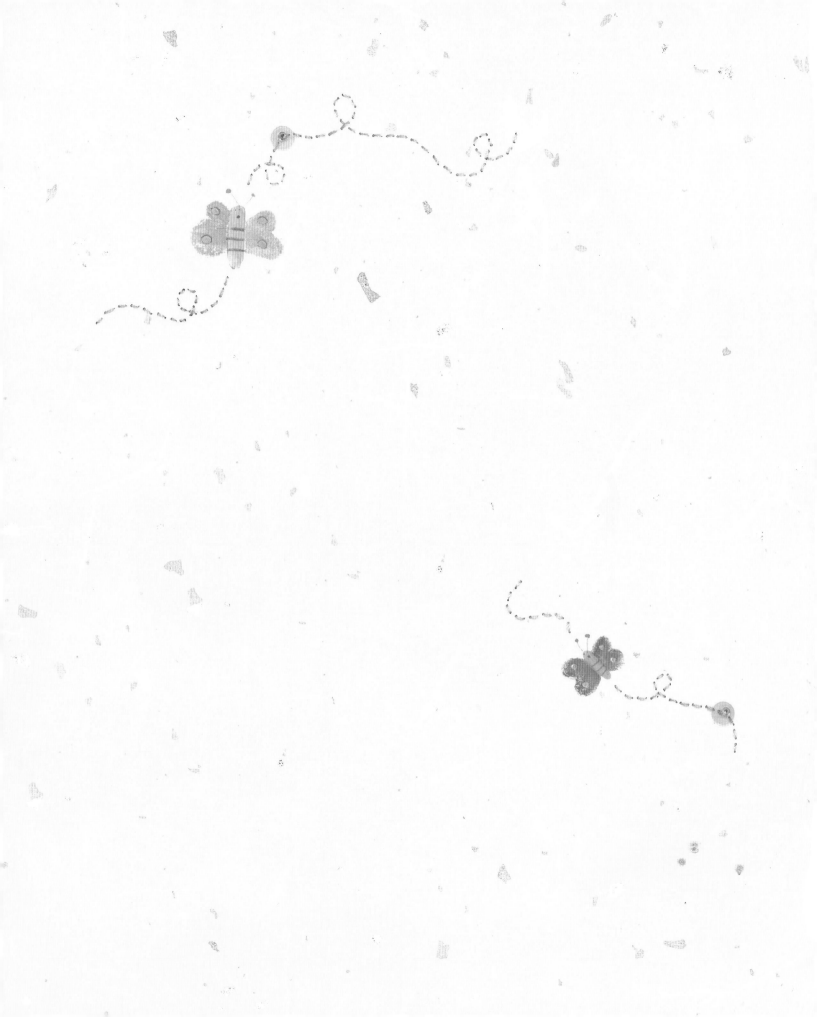